ABOUT THE BANK STREET READY-TO-READ SERIES

More than seventy-five years of educational research, innovative teaching, and quality publishing have earned The Bank Street College of Education its reputation as America's most trusted name in early childhood education.

Because no two children are exactly alike in their development, the Bank Street Ready-to-Read series is written on three levels to accommodate the individual stages of reading readiness of children ages three through eight.

● *Level 1:* GETTING READY TO READ (Pre-K–Grade 1)
Level 1 books are perfect for reading aloud with children who are getting ready to read or just starting to read words or phrases. These books feature large type, repetition, and simple sentences.

● *Level 2:* READING TOGETHER (Grades 1–3)
These books have slightly smaller type and longer sentences. They are ideal for children beginning to read by themselves who may need help.

○ *Level 3:* I CAN READ IT MYSELF (Grades 2–3)
These stories are just right for children who can read independently. They offer more complex and challenging stories and sentences.

All three levels of The Bank Street Ready-to-Read books make it easy to select the books most appropriate for your child's development and enable him or her to grow with the series step by step. The levels purposely overlap to reinforce skills and further encourage reading.

We feel that making reading fun is the single most important thing anyone can do to help children become good readers. We hope you will become part of Bank Street's long tradition of learning through sharing.

The Bank Street College of Education

For Alexandra Rachel
— J.O.

For a free color catalog describing Gareth Stevens' list of high-quality books and multimedia programs, call 1-800-542-2595 (USA) or 1-800-461-9120 (Canada). Gareth Stevens Publishing's Fax: (414) 225-0377.
See our catalog, too, on the World Wide Web: http://gsinc.com

Library of Congress Cataloging-in-Publication Data

Oppenheim, Joanne.
    The show-and-tell frog / by Joanne Oppenheim; illustrated by Kate Duke.
      p.　cm. -- (Bank Street ready-to-read)
    Summary: Allie finds a frog for show-and-tell, but he disappears before she can take him to school.
    ISBN 0-8368-1762-1 (lib. bdg.)
    [1. Show-and-tell presentations--Fiction.　2. Frogs--Fiction.　3. Schools--Fiction]
I. Duke, Kate, ill.　II. Title.　III. Series.
PZ7.O616Sh　1998
[E]--dc21
                                                    97-28943

This edition first published in 1998 by
Gareth Stevens Publishing
1555 North RiverCenter Drive, Suite 201
Milwaukee, Wisconsin 53212 USA

Printed in Mexico

1 2 3 4 5 6 7 8 9 02 01 00 99 98

The Show-and-Tell Frog

by Joanne Oppenheim
Illustrated by Kate Duke

A Byron Preiss Book

Gareth Stevens Publishing
MILWAUKEE

On Sunday, Allie found a green frog.
"Frog," she said, "you are going
to school with me.
You will be my show-and-tell frog!"

That night Allie put holes in a box
and put her frog inside.

She put the box under her bed.

But when Allie woke up
on Monday morning
the box was empty.
"My show-and-tell frog is gone!"
she cried.

Allie searched under her bed.

She looked behind the curtains

and inside her closet.

She could not find her frog
anywhere.

"Frog!" she said. "Where are you?"

"Allie!" her mom called.
"Where are you?"
"I'm right here," Allie called.
She did not want to tell her mom
that the frog was lost.

"Allie!" her mom called again.
"You will be late!"

"I'm coming," called Allie.
She grabbed her backpack.

Allie ran to the bus stop.
There was her friend Christopher.
He was carrying a big bag.
"What's in the bag?" Allie asked.

"Shells," said Christopher.
"I found them at the beach.
They are for show-and-tell.
Do you want to see them?"
"Sure," said Allie.

"Nice shells," Allie said.
"I found something, too.
But I lost it."

Just then the bus pulled up.
Christopher and Allie got on.

Allie sat next to her friend Jenny.
"Look what my grandpa made
for me," said Jenny.
"Wow," said Allie.
"That's a neat ring!
Can I try it on?"
"No," said Jenny.
"It's for show-and-tell.
I don't want to lose it."
Allie understood.
She wished she had not
lost her show-and-tell frog.

Allie got off the bus.
She bumped into her friend Annie.

"Watch it!" Annie yelled.
"You made me spill
my strawberries!
They are for show-and-tell!"
"I'll help pick them up,"
said Allie.
"This is a show-and-taste!"

Allie held the door for Annie.
The red strawberries
were a good show-and-tell.

But Allie wished she had
her show-and-tell frog.

Benjy had the first show-and-tell.
Allie liked the poster
Benjy got at the zoo.

She liked the pictures
Lisa showed of her baby brother.
Having a baby brother
would be fun,
Allie was thinking, when...

she felt something strange
brush against her leg.
"What's that?" yelled Jenny.

"Watch out!" screamed Annie.
"Help!" yelled Benjy.

"What's going on?"
asked the teacher.
"I've got it!" yelled Christopher.
"Get it out of here!" hollered Jenny.

30

"No! No! It's mine!"
shouted Allie.

Allie took her frog and
walked to the front of the class.
She said...

"This is my show-and-tell—
I mean,
my lost and found,
show-and-tell frog!"